Cthulhu w
to claim the Earth ai
The Great (
upon Humankii
Cthulhu has aeemea ii necessary
to prepare Humankind for his coming
Thus, Cthulhu now answers humanity's questions
to help them better themselves.

Dear Cthulhu,

I've been bulimic for years. My well-meaning family and friends are constantly pestering me with misplaced concerns about my eating habits, health, and so on. It is so very annoying, but they refuse to stop. I'm on my fifth intervention.

Ironically, I don't throw up my meals out of a desire to stay thin. I already am. I do it because I love the taste of my own vomit. I'm a gastric acid junkie. I've actually thrown up food just to swallow it again and savor the flavor.

I've never shared this with anyone because I'm worried that they'll think I'm nuts. I'd just like to get all these people to stop bugging me.

Any suggestions?

-Regurgaeater in Rock Bay

Dear Regurgaeater,

Try to limit your hobby to one meal a day. Fill up on nutrition shakes, which will help you gain weight. If you are heavier, your loved ones will assume you have stopped your bulimic ways.

Have you considered medication? There are many on the market with gastric reflux as a side effect. Taking them would allow you to savor your favorite taste almost constantly. Do some research to find out which pill is most likely to cause the reflux then find out what condition it treats. Then fake the illness, go to your physician and have her prescribe it for you. Bon Appetit.

HAVE A DARK DAY

Katy,
Have a
Dark Day!

[signature]

The Collected Advice Columns of **DEAR CTHULHU**

Vol. 1

PATRICK THOMAS

PADWOLF
PUBLISHING

PADWOLF PUBLISHING INC.
WWW.PADWOLF.COM
www.facebook.com/Padwolf

WWW.PATTHOMAS.NET
www.facebook.com/PatrickThomasAuthor

HAVE A DARK DAY
The Collected Advice Columns of Dear Cthulhu Vol. 1
© 2009, 2018 Patrick Thomas

Portions of this book have appeared in column form in the following magazines: Abyss & Apex, Blood Moon Rising, Cthulhu Sex, Dig This Real, Nth Degree, Nth Zine, Space & Time Online, Trails Of Indiscretion, and Werewolf Magazine.

Cover Art by Patrick Thomas and Roy Mauritsen

Cover Design by Roy Mauritsen

Dear Cthulhu is © & TM Patrick Thomas

Special thanks to Dr. Howard Margolin for finding that which others did not.

ISBN 10 digit 1-890096-61-X and 13 digit 978-1-890096-61-8
Third printing. Printed in the USA

If you have any additional questions that Cthulhu can answer, and Cthulhu can answer all questions, Dear Cthulhu welcomes letters and questions at DearCthulhu@dearcthulhu.com. All letters become the property of Dear Cthulhu and may be used in future columns. Sending financial offerings along with your questions is not necessary but is always appreciated.

Anyone foolish enough to follow Dear Cthulhu's advice does so at their own peril.

HAVE A DARK DAY

The Collected Advice Columns of DEAR CTHULHU

Vol. 1

Katy,
Have a
Dark Day!

PATRICK THOMAS

PADWOLF
PUBLISHING

PADWOLF PUBLISHING INC.
WWW.PADWOLF.COM
www.facebook.com/Padwolf

WWW.PATTHOMAS.NET
www.facebook.com/PatrickThomasAuthor

HAVE A DARK DAY
The Collected Advice Columns of Dear Cthulhu Vol. 1
© 2009, 2018 Patrick Thomas

Portions of this book have appeared in column form in the following magazines: Abyss & Apex, Blood Moon Rising, Cthulhu Sex, Dig This Real, Nth Degree, Nth Zine, Space & Time Online, Trails Of Indiscretion, and Werewolf Magazine.

Cover Art by Patrick Thomas and Roy Mauritsen

Cover Design by Roy Mauritsen

Dear Cthulhu is © & TM Patrick Thomas

Special thanks to Dr. Howard Margolin for finding that which others did not.

ISBN 10 digit 1-890096-61-X and 13 digit 978-1-890096-61-8
Third printing. Printed in the USA

If you have any additional questions that Cthulhu can answer, and Cthulhu can answer all questions, Dear Cthulhu welcomes letters and questions at DearCthulhu@dearcthulhu.com. All letters become the property of Dear Cthulhu and may be used in future columns. Sending financial offerings along with your questions is not necessary but is always appreciated.

Anyone foolish enough to follow Dear Cthulhu's advice does so at their own peril.

For Michael Amorel, Edie Collins, Wendy Delmater, Brian Koscienski, Michael D. Pederson, Al J. Vermette, and Hildy Silverman for publishing the Dear Cthulhu columns...

Not that he gave them much choice.

And for Ann Landers and Dear Abby, the best of the best, for blazing the way.

Dear Cthulhu,

My boyfriend "Jim" and I have been seeing each other for 4 months. Things have been going great. Jim tells me he loves me and I know I care for him a lot. Our making out has always been hot and heavy. Jim's a great kisser, but lately, Jim's been wanting to go beyond necking and petting. I'm just not sure I'm ready to give him my virginity. Jim says if I really love him I'll make love to him. My mother always told me if a guy truly loved me, he'll wait until I'm ready and not pressure me.

My friends all think he's really hot and I should do him. I'm the only one of my girlfriends still a virgin, although I have one gay guy friend who still is.

What should I do?

-Confused Virgin in Vermont

Dear Confused,

Virginity is a sacred, beautiful thing and any man who would pressure you to destroy such a rare treasure is a cad you would be better off without. As for your so-called girlfriends, they sound like a bunch of twits.

Remember, it is better to be a leader of men than a follower. The only one you should ever follow is of course Great Cthulhu.

Speaking of which some followers... rather friends of mine are throwing a ritual sacrifice... um, I mean party shortly when the heavens align. How would you like to be the guest of honor? We would love to have you. E-mail me at virgins@dearcthulhu.com. And bring a dish to pass.

Dear Cthulhu,

My next-door neighbor "Dan" and I had always gotten along well until recently. It all started when Dan bought a Doberman and it's been nothing but trouble since. My children are afraid to walk past Dan's house because they're afraid the dog will attack them. Dan leaves it outside and it barks at all hours of the night, keeping my wife and I up. We've been so tired it's affecting our performance at work.

We've asked Dan again and again to do something, anything— in the dog in the backyard and bring it in at night, but he refuses every time.

To top it all off, Dan had borrowed my drill set and hasn't returned it yet and our cat Fluffy is missing.

Would I be justified in killing the dog? And what should I do with the corpse?

-Barking Mad in Baltimore

Dear Barking,

Of course, you would be justified in slaughtering this annoyance. The creature is affecting your sleep, mental health, livelihood and worse of all the safety of your offspring. Consider that compared to you–a human–a dog is a lower life form, much as you humans are to we Great Old Ones, so by right you hold the power of life and death over it.

I recommend barbecuing the canine and inviting your neighbor to partake. It is always best to mend fences or completely annihilate those you share borders with. It's been my experience that most humans not in a position of power tend to lack the drive to wipe out their enemies, so I recommend the former.

Whether you decide to share the source of the meat with Dan is your decision. I suggest not, unless he continues to be a nuisance. Wait until you are losing an argument and drop this bombshell. Then you will not only get the last word but the last laugh as well.

Dear Cthulhu,

I've been spiritually adrift for years since the death of Finny, my goldfish. We were very close and I don't get out much.

I've tried out many of the big religions–Christianity, Buddhism, the Unification Church of Reverend Moon–and several kinds of paganism including Wicca and Wotanism. I even joined the Second Church of Ishtar, but they wouldn't let me attend the orgies, so I quit. None of them were able to give me what I need.

I understand your cult has been growing of late. What do you have to offer worshipers?

Also, since I flushed Finny, I haven't been able to use the toilet in my apartment because I feel like I'd be desecrating her final resting place. Instead, I've made the commode into a shrine, complete with pictures of Finny and I together when she was alive. I even put her favorite castle in the bowl. I've had to run down the street to use the restroom at a nearby gas station. This is a less than optimal solution, as the attendants have been complaining that the bathroom is for customers only and I never buy anything. (I used to buy Finny's fish food there, but I obviously have no need for more. My counter-argument is that they owe me the use of the facilities for all those purchases, plus a candy bar I bought two years ago. Luckily, I always save all my receipts.) The biggest problem is they close at 10 PM and sometimes nature calls in the wee hours of the morning and the garbage disposal in the kitchen sink has its limitations.

I've thought about moving, but the apartment is rent controlled.
Any suggestions?
-Searching in Seattle

Dear Searching,

First off, The Cult of Cthulhu is the 12th fastest growing religion in the world. This is especially impressive since we don't advertise or recruit door to door like say the Jehovah Witnesses. We offer devotees the chance to bring death and chaos to a troubled world. Or possibly end all life on Earth, depending on my mood that day. Plus, everyone gets a spiffy hooded robe to wear to all sacrifices, ceremonies, and socials. We also offer free chanting lessons and Necronomicon study classes. And because we're number 12 we work that much harder.

Sadly, after reading about your issues regarding desecration, I'm just not sure you would be a good fit for us. However, our members, particularly the newer ones, always need practice on the correct way to do a ritual sacrifice. We certainly don't want their first time to be during that limited time the stars are in correct alignment. A single wrong cut could ruin the entire ceremony, so we insist on constant rehearsal so we are always looking for volunteers. Truthfully, we prefer willing participants, because it saves us the time and trouble it would take to go out and kidnap them. Most of my worshipers do have day jobs after all.

On the bonus side for you, I promise you that we'll be able to reunite you with your beloved Finny and would the Great Cthulhu lie?

Dear Cthulhu,

I have a job cleaning out cages at the zoo and have worked here for years. Six months ago, I asked for a raise, which my employer refused. In order to get what I deserve, I came up with a way to make more money.

I opened a brothel at the zoo. The animals are drugged and restrained for safety. There's been a huge response. I now own 3 houses and 2 BMW's. I've also become an internet porn mogul by broadcasting video of the trans-species couples to my thousands of subscribers.

Last week, we had our first accident. One customer had requested the king of beasts for his tryst and I delivered. He knew about the cameras and was hamming things up for the home viewers. He decided to put his head in the lion's mouth and it wasn't the one with the eyes and ears. The lion wasn't groggy enough and bit down. The guy's manhood was completely severed. To make matters worse, the lion didn't spit, he swallowed.

I suggested that we let nature take its course, but "Stubby" refused to wait. We gave the lion a regurgitant and he threw it up. Most of it anyway. The emergency room surgeons were able to reattach it, but it's significantly smaller and chewed up around the edges.

Now Stubby is suing me, but I say it's his own fault. He even signed a waiver release beforehand. What should I do?

-Zoo Pimp in the Bronx

Dear Pimp,

Cthulhu is not a lawyer—there are limits to how evil even I will be—but I do have a suggestion. The video of this incident is a gold mine. In place of litigation and damages, offer Stubby a percentage of gross sales. You will both be millionaires and he will be a celebrity.

How is the lion by the way? I know sometimes humans give me bad gas.

Dear Cthulhu,

Why are you constantly haunting me? Day and night, I hear you whispering, constantly talking inside my head. I can't sleep or work.

What did I ever do to you? And why do you tell me the sports, traffic, and weather?

-Tormented in Toronto

Dear Taunted.

It is not Cthulhu speaking to you, although if it was it would be something for a worthless human as yourself to celebrate, not complain about. I advise you to see your dentist. I would guess one of your fillings is picking up radio broadcasts.

Dear Cthulhu,

I'm a very well-endowed woman (a D cup) and I enjoy wearing sexy tops. My philosophy is if you got it flaunt it. Unfortunately, when I wear something even mildly revealing men stare at my chest. I'm convinced that since the men in the office look me in the boobs instead of the eyes when we talk, that they can't recognize me when I cover up and wear a coat.

Why won't men understand that I dress like this because it makes me feel good, not to titillate or give them a cheap thrill. The women are even worse, calling me a slut and I'm anything but. (Not counting last year's Christmas party of course. I was pretty drunk and didn't realize those guys were twins. I thought I was just seeing double.)

What can I do to get men to look at me above the neckline and realize I'm a real person?

-Tweedle D-cup in Denver

Dear D,

I feel your pain. Whenever I'm out in public, people stare at my facial tentacles and my wings, not to mention the green skin. So few people realize there more to Cthulhu that being a destroyer and an agent of darkness. I collect coins and love puppies, usually with a little Hollandaise sauce.

My first suggestion would be to cover up, but it sounds like that's not what you want. Try placing a mirror in the depths of your cleavage at an angle so anyone staring there will see their own eyes staring back. The effect should be disconcerting enough to stop the behavior, at least temporarily.

Have you considered trying to make money from the situation by renting ad space on your breasts? Make up some temporary tattoos or use body paint to put the ads on.

Or you could do what Cthulhu does. If somebody stares at my tentacles long enough to make me uncomfortable, I use my tentacles to strangle the offender. Perhaps you can train with a martial arts master to develop a new style, using spinning and jumping to maneuver your large mamilaries to knock the offender out or at least give him a couple of black eyes.

Dear Cthulhu,

My boyfriend "Don" and I have been dating for 7 years and I'm itching so much I'm scratching myself raw. I was brought up in a strict family and went to Catholic school, so when Don and I started going together, I told him I wanted to wait. He was fine with it, which made me thrilled with him. That was then and this is now. I'm not thrilled anymore and I'm sick of waiting.

In all that time, he's never even tried anything. I've got a nice figure and think I'm good looking. I've tried dropping hints, wearing sexy outfits and still nothing. I haven't actually come out and said anything–that religious upbringing–but I'm thinking I should.

I care about him and he's put in the time, so I'd like him to be the first, but I can't wait much longer. I keep pulling out wires so the cable guy will stop by and send myself special deliveries to talk to the mailman.

It's beginning to make me wonder if there is something wrong with me.

-Good Girl Ready to Go Bad

Dear Ready,

There are several things wrong with you as far as Cthulhu is concerned, including the fact that you are part of a religion that does not worship me.

This particular problem lays more likely lies with your boyfriend. From my knowledge of human males, it narrows the answer down to certain probabilities. Don may be gay or a eunuch, or a straight woman in drag hiding out from certain factions of organized crime.

I suggest you auction off your virginity on E-bay. I'm sure you will have plenty of takers. It will end your waiting, plus you'll pick up some extra cash.

Dear Cthulhu,

I recently had a very traumatic experience at the dentist's office. Two days ago, I had a root canal and was put under. I came out of the gas early, only to see the dentist getting off of me. His pants were at his ankles and it was obvious what he had done.

I'm understandably upset, but I can help but wonder if it's karma. You see, a couple of weekends before a couple of guys gave me a hundred bucks to put drugs in my girlfriend's drink so they could get with her. Normally, I would have told them to buzz off, but I really wanted to get one of those new U-pod MP3 players, so I did it.

Do you think this is my karmic payback?

-Going Around While Others Come Around

Dear Going,

Probably. The universe has a perverse sense of humor and you got what you deserved.

But what about your dentist? Does he get off scot-free? Cthulhu thinks not. You can be the instrument of Karma instead of its victim.

Call Dr. Loose Pants and share with him what you remember, then tell him you were a virgin and now you're pregnant. Blackmail him for all you can get by promising to go for a DNA test once the baby's born.

After the check clears, report that you made a mistake and were just late. And tape all your conversations in case you need more money down the road.

Dear Cthulhu,

I have a job and a boss that I hate. The slime bag treated me like crap, so I took my revenge by peeing in his coffee pot every morning. It seemed like a good idea at the time, but it ended up backfiring on me. It turns out he loved my "special blend" and couldn't get enough of it. He told the entire office and they loved it too. I'm not really sure why, but I am diabetic which is supposed to make the urine sweet. That or they were all just used to really horrible coffee.

Without telling me, my idiot boss entered my brew in a contest that Spacebucks Coffeehouse was running to find the best new coffee. I won and they offered me a ton of money to manage one of their biggest shops and make my special blend for the customers.

I'm torn. I could use the money and it would be a huge relief to get out of this office. What should I do?

-A Real Pisser In Pittsburgh

Dear Pisser,

Take the job, but insist on your own private office to make the coffee. And remember to drink lots of fluids.

Dear Cthulhu,

My partner and I recently went pro at women's beach volleyball. We made it to the finals, but the competition was fierce. I was worried they'd beat us. I knew whoever won that tournament would also get a bikini endorsement and I wanted that money, so when the opportunity came to drug our opponents drinks right before the match, I took it.

We won, two games to one.

The only problem is, now I feel guilty. Suggestions?

-Setter in Seattle

Dear Setter,

I can understand why you would feel guilty. The other team was drugged and it still took you three games to beat them. Not only should you feel guilty, you should be ashamed.

I suggest that next time you consider using stronger drugs or train harder. Probably both.

Dear Cthulhu,

I'm a newlywed and I have a secret which is hammering a wedge between me and my husband "Fred". I was in a porno and I really don't want him to find out, especially since I sort of filmed it on the morning of our wedding. The way I figured it, a lot of girls have a last fling before taking the marital plunge. Instead of forking out good money to a stripper, I just managed to get paid for mine. Plus, it was before the ceremony, so technically I didn't break any vows.

There was one other thing. Since we rented the hall for the day and the ceremony was in the afternoon, I sublet it to the production company. Between that and my salary for starring in the video, I paid off the wedding and the honeymoon, although Fred thinks I got the money from my parents. Those cheapskates would give me a cent, so I really didn't have much of a choice.

My worry is that Fred will find out, but I was smart enough to wear a disguise. Sort of. The film was titled The Bride Of Sexenstein, so I was able to wear my veil the entire time. For someone who didn't know me intimately, like my husband's friends, it would be enough. I did make the mistake of wearing the same dress for both the movie and the wedding, but I figured the odds of a guy noticing that while watching porn is pretty low.

I had intended for it to be a one-time deal, but I'm up for some award, a kind of porno Oscar. The producers have approached me to do the sequel— The Ex-Wife of Sexenstein. Again, normally, I'd say no, but we're looking to buy a house and they added a zero to the end of what they paid me last time. It would practically pay off the entire mortgage. My main problem is because I'm married now, I'd technically be cheating on Fred and that bothers me. Of course, so does living in the cramped one bedroom apartment we're in now.

Help me prioritize—which is more important, my vows or paying off our house?

-Adult Star in Albany

Dear Star,

Your vows are paramount of course. A promise given should not be broken. I would kill if an acolyte broke their vows to me.

Of course, there is a way to do both. Divorce him, make the film, and then remarry him. Just make sure at his second stag party they have strippers, not films. Your veil would probably not be enough to fool him.

Dear Cthulhu,

Have you ever had plastic surgery?
-Nosey Nosejober in Silicon Valley

Dear Nosejober,

No, but I had a plastic surgeon for lunch last week. Sadly, he looked much better than he tasted, which seemed somehow appropriate.

Dear Cthulhu,

I've been bulimic for years. My well-meaning family and friends are constantly pestering me with misplaced concerns about my eating habits, health, and so on. It is so very annoying, but they refuse to stop. I'm on my fifth intervention.

Ironically, I don't throw up my meals out of a desire to stay thin. I already am. I do it because I love the taste of my own vomit. I'm a gastric acid junkie. I've actually thrown up food just to swallow it again and savor the flavor.

I've never shared this with anyone because I'm worried that they'll think I'm nuts. I'd just like to get all these people to stop bugging me.

Any suggestions?

-Regurgaeater in Rock Bay

Dear Regurgaeater,

Try to limit your hobby to one meal a day. Fill up on nutrition shakes, which will help you gain weight. If you are heavier, your loved ones will assume you have stopped your bulimic ways.

Have you considered medication? There are many on the market with gastric reflux as a side effect. Taking them would allow you to savor your favorite taste almost constantly. Do some research to find out which pill is most likely to cause the reflux then find out what condition it treats. Then fake the illness, go to your physician and have her prescribe it for you. Bon Appetit.

Dear Cthulhu,

Hey, tentacled dude! Greetings from the Tri-Omegas at State U! You rock Ancient dude!

We have a very important question for you, one that could affect our lives here forever.

What's your favorite drinking game? You could come and play it with us at one of our keggers.

-Veni, Vidi, Vino (I came, I saw, I drank)

Dear Vino,

My favorite by far is "spin the bottle". Instead of sucking face with the human it points at, I suck out their soul. It simply takes things to the next level as far as I'm concerned.

Thank you for the invitation. I will attend. Think you can fix me up with a couple dozen sorority girls?

Dear Cthulhu.

I've been married to "Mandy", the most wonderful woman in the world for 9 years. Unfortunately, for the last 3, she's been in a coma. This has made life very difficult for me. I visit the hospital every day, which after you figure in work, commuting, and sleep, just doesn't leave time for much else. The doctors say she probably won't come out of it and I don't have the heart to pull her feeding tube.

The truth of the matter is I still have needs that aren't being met. Manly needs. My family and friends have told me that I should start dating, but I take my marriage vows very seriously and I can't cheat on my wife, even if she's in a coma. At the same time, two little round parts of me were blue and ready to turn purple, so I came up with a compromise.

I had sex with my comatose wife. The first time was a little awkward I admit, but it got easier. When she was up and about, we usually had sex three times a week, so I've made sure I limited it to that many times now, so I wouldn't be taking advantage of the situation. Except for the week of my birthday when I always got a special present, although it was hard to do with all those tubes in her mouth. But hey, I figured we are married after all, so it's okay.

Things went well for months, that is until last week. A routine blood test showed that Mandy was pregnant. We had never used a condom before and I hadn't thought to start now, which in hind-sight was probably a mistake. It makes sense that they'd stop giving Mandy her birth control pills all things considered. Now there is an investigation at the hospital to find out how this happened. Everyone from the doctors and nurses to the hospital administration has been apologizing to me. I think they're afraid I'm going to sue them. They were thrilled when I agreed not to talk to the newspapers.

The biggest downside is now they have video surveillance of my wife 24/7, so our midnight trysts are over.

I'm worried they might charge someone else falsely with the crime. What should I do—confess to the crime or wait and see how thing turn out? The last complicating factor is if they charge someone else, will I still get to keep the baby? If the issue comes up, should I insist on a paternity test or would that get me in more trouble? The truth is Mandy and I always wanted children. I'm just not sure if I'm ready to be a single father. Do you think what I did was wrong? And can you come up with a way for me to be with my wife again romantically without getting caught by the cameras?

-Comaphilic Husband In Conklin

Dear Comaphilic,

You say you are not sure you are ready for the responsibilities of single fatherhood. Frankly, you should have thought about that before you procreated with your unconscious spouse. You had to know the possible consequences and let us be honest, it is not like you can plead the typical human defense that it was in the heat of the moment.

As you say, you and Mandy are married so I do not feel what you did was wrong. However, if Mandy ever wakes up she may feel differently, as might the local authorities.

I recommend that you confess nothing. Say you want to raise your wife's child as your own and custody should not be a problem. Play your cards right and the hospital may give you an out of court settlement that will set you and your child up for life.

As for the paternity test, I say do not do it, at least publicly. Let us be honest here, Mandy is not the same woman now as when you married her. How do you know for sure that you are the father? Someone else could have just as easily had relations with your wife when you were not there, although Cthulhu suggests if she did, that you do not blame her. Have the test done at a private clinic. If you are the father, congratulations. If not, then you can use the results to get a larger settlement by threatening to go to the press. In the current health care market, that kind of publicity could ruin their business, so they will probably go along with whatever you ask for just to keep you quiet.

As for copulating with your unconscious spouse with the security in place, may I recommend waiting for a blackout and hoping their generators are only hooked up to the lifesaving equipment.

Dear Cthulhu,

You are without a doubt the most evil, heinous creature in the entire world and a total waste of life. Why anyone would print your rantings is a mystery to me.

-Outraged In Ohio

Dear Outraged,

Thank you for your kind words. It is always so nice to get fan mail.

Dear Cthulhu,

I've recently become engaged to a wonderful man, but there is something I'm not telling him. Up until six months before I met him, I was a man and having been a man I know how angry some guys can get if they find this stuff by accident. The main reason I haven't told him is that I'm afraid of losing him.

I feel I can justify never telling him because up until three years before that I was a woman who felt she was really a man. After I had my first sex change, I realized I had made a mistake and was just trying to tick off my parents. After they died in a bizarre ostrich stampede accident, I decided to become a woman again. I moved clear across the country so nobody here should ever know I was briefly a man. If it ever comes up, I can prove I was born a woman-I have childhood pictures, my high school yearbook, prom photos. But there is always the issue of honesty. Can a relationship based on a lie ever endure?

-Gender Bender Againder

Dear Bender,

No human relationship can ever endure. The best you can hope for is 70-80 years. As for honesty, I find it grossly overrated, but you can tell him the truth without him catching on. Tell him you were born a woman but went through an experimental stage where you dated women. Many human males will find this a turn on and ask to bring another female into your procreative activities. If you agree to it on a regular basis, it is my experience that a male human will overlook almost anything else.

Dear Cthulhu,

I was helping an upper middle-class couple out by being a surrogate mother and carrying their child. True they only asked me because I'm on welfare and they figured I'd jump at the money. I don't mind because they were right. I was more than willing to be pregnant for 10 grand, plus medical and rent.

The problem is I lost the baby. My own fault, I guess for riding the Rolling Death roller coaster 32 times in the same day. I guess they really mean it when they put up those signs saying pregnant women shouldn't ride.

I haven't told them because at the very least they'd stop paying my rent. I'm pretty sure they won't pay me my money now too.

I came up with a solution. My friend "Cassie" is pregnant and was going to get an abortion. I talked her out of it and had her move in with me. I offered to split the money with her if she gives her baby to this couple. She's due three weeks before I was, so I figure we'll just say the baby was early. She goes to the doctor, pretending she's me so the couple pays for it. I've even given them Cassie's ultrasound picture and padded my stomach to pretend I'm pregnant. The best part is I told Cassie they were only paying me 5 grand, so I get to keep $7,500 for myself.

I think I have all the angles covered, but wanted an expert opinion. Have I missed anything?

-Baby Broker in Boston

Dear Broker,

You seem to be adaptable and sneaky, even for a human. It is a very good plan, so long as you can keep the couple from going to the OB/GYN doctor with you. The only possible crimp is the ethnic makeup of the parties involved. Now from Cthulhu's point of view, you all look alike, but many humans are very particular about these matters, hating each other for differences in skin tone without realizing they are more alike than different. It does help keep them from bothering with my plans, so I do not complain. Are the couple the same background as Cassie? What about her baby's father? Will the baby be able to pass? If so, you have a good chance of succeeding. Otherwise, the couple may balk, not pay you, and probably turn you into the authorities for fraud.

Also, don't let Cassie see the check or she may catch on and if she backs out, your plan falls apart.

.

Dear Cthulhu,

I'm a first-year medical student at a prestigious university and I'm loving it. As part of our training, we have to dissect human cadavers. I'm also in a fraternity. We had a party one weekend with a combo toga/zombie theme. I got this great idea that it would be very cool to have an actual corpse to liven up the place. I figured maybe the guy might like one last party. Besides, I had to pay the school for the cadaver, so I figured he was my property anyway.

The party was awesome, down to the jello shots made in brain molds. Only the next morning when I went to bring "Mort" back to the anatomy lab, he was gone, nowhere to be found.

I admit, I freaked out a bit but my friends kept me sane. I had started to put up MISSING-REWARD signs with Mort's face on them. Luckily, my friends stopped me. Problem was, I knew I'd get expelled if anyone found out what I did. Plus, my parents would kill me. They took out a second mortgage for my tuition.

My frat does a lot of volunteer work with the homeless, so I went downtown to help hand out sandwiches. We went in an alley to give a PBJ to this one guy, but he was stone cold dead under a cardboard box. Then it came to me-I could use his corpse to re-place my cadaver. He had no ID and he was homeless after all, so who'd miss him?

One of my frat brothers is majoring in mortuary science and had a key to the lab. He embalmed the guy for me. I snuck my new cadaver into anatomy lab and worked all night to dissect him to the point of Mort. As we keep the hands, face, & feet covered until we're ready to cut up those parts no one was the wiser. I had gotten away with it.

Or so I thought. Two of our fraternity brothers took a leave of absence the day after the zombie toga party. They won the lottery and decided to drive cross-country. A week later, their first post-card arrived with a picture of Mort in front of the Empire State Building. The next week we got one with him on the beach. One came every week from points nationwide from the Grand Canyon to Mount Rushmore.

It's getting closer to the end of the school year and the pictures are getting closer to home. I figure they'll get back the last week of school with Mort, which will leave me with two bodies.

I've got a 4.0 GPA and don't want it ruined. What should I do?
-I Got Two Bodies in Boise

Dear Two,

You are obviously a bright and hardworking young man. You may do well in spite of this, so there is no reason this mischief should ruin an otherwise promising career. Most Universities are bureaucracies and as such overloaded by paperwork. After the class is finished, find out what cooler they put the bodies in for disposal and simply sneak Mort back in. Whomever is in charge will probably notice the discrepancy of the extra body, but will more than likely quiet it quiet. Reporting it would mean paperwork, investigations, and them most likely being blamed.

Just remember to remove any identifying clothing like togas and shirts with your fraternity name on it.

Dear Cthulhu,

I wrote to you several months ago about my plan to replace the baby I miscarried because of riding too many times on a roller coaster with my friend's unwanted baby. Everything went great. "Cassie" and I got the money—me more than her—and the couple got a baby. Everything was good all around until "Jerome" showed up. Apparently, he was the father of Cassie's baby and he headed for the hills once he heard she was pregnant. Cassie went out and celebrated at the local bar, got a little wasted. Jerome happened to see her spreading a lot of money around and managed to get her to spread something else. You'd think she would have learned after the first time. After the fact, the drunken slut actually told Jerome what we did and now he wants his share! Says if we don't cough it up, he'll sue for custody of the child, which means the couple will want their money back.

I don't know what to do. I don't want to give him any of my money. If anyone pays him, it should be Cassie as she's the one who blabbed. She already spent all of her share, so that option is out. Of course, I could just get him killed for a couple of hundred.

Any suggestions?

-Baby Broker In Boston Worried About Becoming Broke

Dear Broker,

Again to my readers—people should not kill people. That is reserved for Cthulhu and his appointed delegates.

I have a better suggestion. Call his bluff. If Jerome wanted to be a parent, he would not have fled the first time. Explain to him that Cassie signed away all her rights (whether she did or not) and if he wins the baby and the responsibility for raising it to the age of 18 will rest solely on him. The money spent in the first six months will far exceed anything he'd extort from you.

To add the icing to the cake, have Cassie tell him she's pregnant again, so the money would have to go to her for child support anyway. I predict Jerome will bother you no more.

Dear Cthulhu,

I sent you the $2,000 your cult requires to become a minister so I could preside over the wedding of my two best friends. It's been three months and I haven't yet received my certificate in the mail. The wedding is in less than 2 months. Could you please do whatever you can to expedite things or give me my two-grand back?

-The Soon To Be Reverend Smith

Dear Smith,

As I am sure you noticed on your paperwork, the $2,000 is for deacon. A full minister is $5,000, but it is worth it just for the tax breaks. However, my cult is not some mail order scam that will just make anyone a minister. We have additional requirements, which you have not completed. (See Paragraph 17, subsection b on the contract you signed in your blood.) Cthulhu was surprised that you signed without arguing about the vows of celibacy in Paragraph 69. Most of my acolytes insist on taking that part out and Cthulhu is not so much of a monster to not go along with it. Honestly, I have no idea how the Catholics and the Buddhists get new clergy with that requirement. In fact, you are the first non-eunuch to ever sign, so we are happy to have you. Just remember, if you make a mistake and break that vow to me, Cthulhu will get rid of the organ that broke the vow. I doubt there could be a second offense.

My records do show what is holding things up. You have not yet performed the required ritual sacrifice. A full minister has to do 3. If Cthulhu is mistaken, and Cthulhu never is, and you have taken care of this please send proof by way of a video along with the body. If the cost of shipping an entire body is too much of a hardship on you, the heart and liver will suffice. Place them in ice and include some barbecue sauce. And hopefully, for your sake, you were not planning on bringing a date to the wedding.

Dear Cthulhu,

I think you are wonderful, wise, warm, and witty. Just knowing you are out there helping us with our problems makes me feel better about life.

Thank you so much. I will definitely be writing in again to ask for your help.

-Gushing in Galveston

Dear Gushing,

While everything you say is true, I request you get your brown nose out of my tentacles. You obviously want something of Cthulhu but did not have the courage to ask directly. Never darken my mailbox again.

Dear Cthulhu,

I've never had much luck with women, that is until I met "Natasha". She's a very hot woman half my age. We met at a bar. It turns out she recently broke up with her longtime boyfriend and he kicked her out, so she needed a place to stay. I invited her back to my house out of courtesy so she didn't have to sleep on the street. Well, that and the hope that I might get lucky. It hadn't happened in years, not since that drunken night I volunteered at the senior center.

It worked. Natasha moved in and that was 3 months ago. It's been great. However, I have some concerns that she might not really care about me for me. For one thing, she'd been insisting that I put her on the deed as co-owner of my house, which I own outright. She even cut me off and kicked me out of my own bedroom until I did it. I didn't quite feel it was a good idea, so I got the pretend deed from my niece's "Sandy's Dream House" and put her name on that. I didn't even sign my real name. She didn't notice and was much more affectionate after.

Lately, she's been exhibiting some kinky tendencies, including a Santa Claus fetish. Well, that's how it started out, me wearing the red suit and white beard, her sitting on my lap and so on. Then it got weird. She wanted me to dress up like a reindeer, including antlers. Lately, she's been wanting to do it outside in the woods behind my house with me in the costume, after a game of hide and seek. Deer season is coming up and I'm beginning to have suspicions about where her true intentions lie.

What do you think?

-Cupid Taken With Vixen

Dear Taken,

As long as you do not have the desire to visit the afterlife, your course is clear. Go outside for the game, but have her hide. Get all of her stuff together and put it outside, including the reindeer outfit then change the locks.

Wait for her to call the police and she will undoubtedly show them the Dream House deed to show them that she owes half of your home. When they see what it really it, it should be good for some laughs. Then tell them she's been stalking you and pretending that she's your wife. Explain how she puts the stuff outside the door, pretending that the two of you are married. Demand a restraining order.

Do not overly concern yourself with the loss of the frequent procreation. Go out to another bar and mention the restraining order. In my experience, there is a subgroup among human females who will find this attractive. Of course, they are also the type you may really need one for, so don't take them to your home. Use a motel instead.

Dear Cthulhu,

Despite popular opinion, I'm not confused about my sexuality. I'm a bisexual man who loves both genders equally and has never quite been satisfied with either by itself. Threesomes are enjoyable, but inevitably the other two members notice one another, then try to satisfy each other and frankly sex should be all about me. It's a point I've never been adequately been about to get across to my many, many partners.

I started looking for love with transsexuals, both pre- and post-op, but the truth is most of them were even more messed up than I was. Plus, I hate fake enhancements, boobs and penises equally.

Cupid finally struck me over the head with his anvil and I fell in love at the carnival. More specifically the freak show. They had Deb-Bo, a half-man, half woman and it was love at first sight. For me at least. I figured it must be a trick, like the living mermaid or the snakeboy, so I waited until after dark when the carnival closed and followed Deb-Bo back to a trailer. I spied in the window until Deb-Bo got changed for bed. I almost fell over when I saw Deb-Bo's divine nakedness before me. I found the Holy Grail. Deb-Bo was a living, breathing hermaphrodite! No fake surgical enhancements here. Just glorious one hundred percent pure fusion of the genders.

Figuring knocking on her trailer in the middle of the night was not the best way to her heart or her bed, I left to return the next day. I tried to woo her—I brought flowers, candy, membership in the steak of the month club, even the finest hermaphroditic porn I could find on short notice. Deb-Bo was not impressed. In fact, Deb-Bo went so far as to have the Lizard-Man and the strong man throw me out.

I'm not one to take no for an answer, so I broke into Deb-Bo's trailer to wait and make my pitch again. When that vision of loveliness opened the door, I was in the bedroom ready to seduce my hermaphrodite, waiting naked with a guitar. I guess Deb-Bo didn't like ABBA because I was greeted by screams and attempted fleeing. I was still hurting from where the Lizard-Man had kicked me and had no desire to be manhandled again—unless Deb-Bo was the one doing it of course—so I hit the object of my desire over the head with the guitar. I only wanted to shut my love up, but I ended up knocking Deb-Bo out.

I contemplated taking Deb-Bo then and there, but couldn't bring myself to violate and debase this thing of beauty in that way. I wanted to wait until my vision of loveliness woke up and try and convince Deb-Bo to take me as a lover. I could hear the other carnies going about their business outside and I realized that the trailer would not be the safest place for me to wait. After wiping my fingerprints off everything, I wrapped Deb-Bo in a blanket and carried the hermaphrodite to my car. I got Deb-Bo in and out of the trunk and to my basement without any problems.

I tied Deb-Bo to an old bed and gagged my beauty. When Deb-Bo woke, it wasn't pretty. Instead of the beautiful sexual union I imagined, Deb-Bo tried to claw and bite me.

I'm at a loss. I guess technically I kidnapped her and the police won't accept that following true love's path as a good excuse. The smartest thing to do would be to kill her and get rid of the body, but I can't bring myself to harm this pinnacle of human sexuality. What should I do? How do I make her fall in love with me?

-Bi Guy Who Made A Hermaphrodite Go Bye Bye

Dear Bi,

You have gotten yourself into a bit of a bind. Kidnapping is not something that should be entered into lightly or on the spur of the moment. To be successful takes planning. My acolytes undergo months of training before I let them go out into the community at large to gather new recruits and/or sacrifices.

But in your situation, it is too late for hindsight. I hope you are handy around the house because you need to pay a visit to your nearest home hardware warehouse and purchase the necessary materials to make your basement soundproof and escape proof. Chains are much better than rope, which can be gradually worn away by rubbing on a course surface.

That should help you prevent the object of your obsessions from escaping and turning you in. Now to address your main concern of winning this hermaphrodite's affections. Drugs are only a temporary fix, although using ones that cause an addiction is a common ploy in urban areas to make young females pliable to trading intercourse for more drugs. Unfortunately, if you are not familiar with how the drug culture works, you'll most likely end up getting caught by the authorities, which in turn could lead them to your prisoner. And you are very correct about the pursuit of true love not holding up in court. My using freedom of religion to justify sacrifices only works about half the time. And then mostly in California.

I recommend researching Stockholm Syndrome, either at your local library or via the internet. This is a common condition where hostages begin to empathize with and gain sympathy and even affection for their captors. After enough research, you should be able to work toward inducing this in your captive intended. If you work things correctly with this brainwashing Deb-Bo may end up willingly offering herself to you.

Dear Cthulhu,

My wife is cheating on me. I figured it out when I found a half dozen used condoms in our bathroom garbage. When I confronted her, she told me the man she was screwing around with is a hitman for the mob and if I say anything or file for divorce, she'll send him after me.

I've lost every fight I've ever been in and don't even own a gun, so going after him myself would be suicide. Obviously, so would leaving her.

I'm worried that if I kill my wife that either the cops will put me in jail or my wife's lover will put me in cement booties in the nearest body of water.

What can I do?

-Cuckolded in Connecticut

Dear Cuckolded,

Normally Cthulhu is opposed to humans killing each other, a right which should be Cthulhu's alone, but above that is the sanctity of vows. Without that, my followers might feel they could just leave my service or think for themselves and then where would things be? And a human who flaunts his heretic behavior of taking lives that ultimately belong to Cthulhu is certainly an abomination before me. In light of this, I am giving you dispensation to end their vow breaking lives. As you sound like a devout coward, I recommend lacing their condoms with poison, both inside and out. Using superglue on both the interior and exterior of the prophylactics will help ensure they do not get away before the poison does its job. And it seems somehow appropriate for a hitman to go out with a bang.

Dear Cthulhu,

I'm obsessed with fighting. Not physically doing it myself, of course. I'm rather small and the only exercise I get is playing video games. My biceps may be puny, but my thumbs are massive. I was wondering who you think would win in a cage match between a dragon and a mech warrior?

-Nerdalicious In Nantucket

Dear Nerdalicious,

You need to get out. There is more to life than wondering how some imaginary fight would turn out. In fact, if you are interested in the real thing my cult has fight night the third Tuesday of every month. We like to put different species up against each other while we nosh. It is available on Internet pay-per-view of course.

In answer to your question, the mech would have the advantage in a cage match since it would have greater mobility. In the open, with the element of surprise and mech armor that was built by the lowest builder, the dragon would have the advantage. And since you have chosen to waste my valuable time with this inane question, Cthulhu insists you make it up to me up. Since you feel your thumbs are so massive, I invite you to thumb wrestle in a cage match on our next fight night against all comers. Of course, the tigers, cobras, and pit bulls technically don't have any thumbs, so we may have to improvise. Congratulations on your exclusive lifelong contract with Dear Cthulhu Entertainment. Your new manager has already been dispatched to pick you up. Don't mind the chloroform. We shall deduct its cost from your salary or your death benefits, depending on how your matches go.

Dear Cthulhu,

Great one, I hate to have to tell you this but we are stopping publication of Cthulhu Sex with the next issue and we will no longer require your column. As I know you are now carried in many other magazine and venues, I hope this will not cause any undue hardship on you or any hard feelings between us.

-Most devoutly yours,

St. Michael

Editor-In-Chief Cthulhu Sex magazine

Dear Publishing Coward,

Stopping any way that Cthulhu has of communicating with the masses is completely unacceptable. How will your readers find out when the first volume of the collected Dear Cthulhu comes out in book form sometime next year? As you know when you signed up as one of my followers I claimed not only your soul, but a portion of the profits from your magazine. As my accountants tell me you are making money, this must be because your so-called writing career is becoming successful. For one of my followers to put himself before Cthulhu is the gravest sin and must be punished. Even as I write this, my true followers are on their way to pick you up and bring you to me where I shall show you the error of your selfish ways. Then while you are still alive, I shall flay the skin from your bones. I shall then tan the hide and print a new issue of Cthulhu Sex on the leather, consisting completely of Dear Cthulhu columns and haiku poetry and limericks dedicated to my glory. Then after making you read it aloud on video, I will end your life most painfully. Then I shall marry your intended bride while using rope and a marionette handle to make your corpse dance and act as my best man. I will leave the honeymoon festivities to your imagination, but once a woman goes tentacle she won't ever go back.

Dear Cthulhu,

I'm a writer who is having a lot of trouble getting published. I think I'm good and would sell well if only given a chance, but I just can't get any editors to notice my work. How do you recommend that authors escape from the slush pile?

-Hopeful Wordsmith from Hackensack

Dear Hopeful,

Slush piles are often manned by low-level editors who have taken the job in hopes of furthering their own writing careers only to realize that all the time they spend working on the work of others takes away from the finite time that they themselves have to create stories of their own. Some of these become bitter over their lack of personal writing success, so when they move up they become drunk on the power they have gained over other writers. They make it too difficult to submit by making ridiculous requirements—double-spaced manuscripts except for every thirteenth line which should be triple-spaced except when it is a multiple of 1, in which case it should be single spaced, unless the first word begins with a vowel. Then it should be one and a half spaces. And the open reading period only allows for manuscripts received in pink envelopes at exactly 2:03 AM every other day, excluding those days ending in Y. It is enough to make anyone crazy. Why, if the Necronomicon were written today, Cthulhu does not know if it would be considered publishable. Of course, the first reader would be driven mad, but the question is would anyone in the publishing world even notice the difference?

The key for the writer is to never give up and always work at getting better. Few people know that Lovecraft's first few stories were about fluffy bunnies and smiling ponies. They were not well received, although I did personally enjoy them. Luckily, he got better, found his voice, and you will too. Or the pressure of never being recognized for what you perceive as your greatness will eventually drive you mad, alienating you from family and friends who don't want to read your seventeenth revision of the novel that was based on your "What I Did Over Summer Vacation" essay that you wrote in seventh grade. Things will progress until you start mumbling to yourself, lose your job and end up homeless on the street writing haiku poetry on empty alley walls in chalk you mixed from dirt, discarded flour, and your own blood.

Fortunately for your mental health, there are a few editors and even agents who truly care about the books and stories they publish, who rage against the corporate mindset that insists all work be similar and follow the same formula as their last four bestsellers. True, they tend to be overworked, underpaid, and poorly appreciated, not to mention far behind on their reading, but these few are the hope of every writer trying to get published. They look into the apex of the abyss and when they see something good staring back at them from the slush pile, they smile and bring it into the light. Perhaps it shall one day happen to you.

Dear Cthulhu,

My mother always told me to marry a doctor. I hadn't had much luck in dating anyone from the medical profession until "Dr. Stan". He's a pediatrician with his own practice, so he's quite well off. He's also handsome and young. Sounds perfect, right? It's not.

We had been dating for about two months when he finally took me back to his place. I was thinking this was finally it. He left me in his bedroom and went into the bathroom to change into something more comfortable. I was expecting silk boxers or a robe, maybe a thong. Instead, he comes out in a bonnet and a diaper. I was too shocked for words. While I was still stunned, Dr. Stan asked me to change him. Not knowing what to do, I obliged and got the hell out of there.

I planned never to see him again, but the next day I got a dozen roses and a Rolex. Not the cheap kind either. So when he called me that night to ask for another date, I figured what the heck. He invited me over for a homemade dinner. He met me at the door in a tux, lead me into the dining room. He fed me a five-course meal, with steak and lobster as the main course. He even fed me chocolate covered strawberries for dessert. One thing led to another and I rocked his world. Then he rattled mine. First, he actually cuddled. Then he got up to go to the bathroom and again he came out in his infant gear. He asked me to change him, this time adding powder to the mix. I was in the afterglow, so I obliged. Then he did things to me with a battery powered rattle that I can't even begin to explain but were thoroughly enjoyable. The next morning he paid my apartment lease for three months.

We've been going on like this for a year. I've enjoyed our time, but frankly, I'm embarrassed to tell anybody what we do behind closed doors. Last night he proposed marriage. I haven't given him an answer yet. Being Mrs. Dr. Stan would be prestigious. My mother would be proud and my sister jealous. (She brags that she married a doctor, but he's only a chiropractor.) I'd be financially comfortable, but I'm not sure I want a lifetime of this playacting.

Other than that though, it would be a perfect arrangement.

What should I do?

-Dr. Stan's Hot Mama in Hoboken

Dear Woman,

I cannot tell you how refreshing it is to get a letter that is not all bogged down in emotions like love and caring. Your relationship is based on something much more likely to last—fee for services. Dr. Stan has sensitive needs, which you help fulfill. You, in turn, are rewarded financially for your efforts. Frankly, I say do not worry about what others would think. What two consenting adults do in the privacy of their own bedroom is nobody's business but theirs.

I do advise getting some points clarified first. Will you have a marriage bed or a crib? Make sure you are okay with the answer. Also, you don't mention if you want children. Assuming you do and tending to Dr. Stan does not fill those maternal needs, you should discuss it with him. Does he want children? If so, will he be jealous of the time and attention you will have to give them? Will he fly into a jealous rage if he sees you changing their diapers? When the time comes, you might want to consider counseling or letting him do all the childcare chores until they are potty trained.

Dear Cthulhu,

I'm a big man with a gambling habit. I was in debt to my book-ie "Rocko" for 25 big ones and had no way to pay. I only make minimum wage. Rocko should have had more sense than let me run up that much debt, but I love betting on the ponies. Sadly, it's polo ponies and Rocko's the only bookie who takes bets on the sports of kings.

Rocko came to me with a solution. There was this one rich guy who owed him over a million but wasn't paying. He said if I took care of it, we'd be square. Naturally, I assumed he meant kill the guy, but he wasn't specific in case the area was bugged. I guess I shouldn't have because he just wanted the guy a little hurt and a lot scared to get him to pay.

Now the cops busted Rocko because they found out about the money the stiff owed him. Rocko has been a standup guy and hasn't squealed on me, but I'm worried. His dad is a capo and I'm more worried about his family than I am the cops. I've thought about going to his father and try to explain things.

I'm scared and don't know what to do.

-Life Breaker in Brooklyn

Dear Breaker,

Before I answer, do you suffer from depression? Have you been contemplating suicide? Enjoy swimming with cement footwear? If so, go to his father and throw yourself on his mercy.

Another option would be to go to the cops and confess what you did, thereby getting Rocko freed from jail. However, in my experience with humanity, this type of selfless act only happens among the psychologically challenged population and in sappy television shows and movies.

Your best option is to run away, very far and very fast. Change your name and give up betting on polo. It is unusual enough to make it easy for you to be traced.

Plastic surgery would be a good option as well. If you can't afford to have it done right, may I recommend my pamphlet "DO IT YOURSELF COSMETIC SURGERY." Just send me $14.95 plus $5 shipping and handling. It tells you how to alter your appearance with items you probably have lying around the house. And shows you where to find the best discount cemetery plots in case you screw up.

Dear Cthulhu,

I might as well come right out and say it–I'm not an attractive man, even in the dimmest light. In bright light, my face has been known to frighten small children and animals.

As a kid, my parents wrapped me in raw meat and stopped feeding the dog so she would play with me. Instead, our family pet became anorexic. I really wanted to go to my high school prom, but I couldn't get a date. All the prostitutes I approached wanted more money than I had. I even asked my mother in desperation, but even she was too embarrassed to be seen with me.

My question is how can I get a woman to go out with me? My father suggested drugging them, saying that's how he got Mom. I'm uncomfortable with the idea of date rape and won't do that.

You're not the most attractive of people, what with the facial tentacles, green skin and bat wings, yet from all accounts you have no trouble getting women.

What do you recommend for me to do to get a woman?

-Hideous in Houston

Dear Hideous,

To start with, you do not have my many advantages, but I will do my best to help you.

Let's start with the obvious. Have you ever considered a blind date? I mean that literally. The blind usually do not put such a priority on looks, although I recommend holding off on letting her feel your face until at least the third date in hopes that her getting to know you would help her to not run away screaming. So, if you have no problems with sunglasses, canes and guide dogs, this may be the option for you. However, since you did mention your effect on animals, it may be best to steer toward women with canes only, because nothing ruins a romantic evening quite like an animal whining in terror. Believe me, I know.

Should this fail, your only other real option is power. Women are drawn to it and some of them are willing to overlook certain things–infidelity, lack of sexual prowess, murder, and even looks–to be with a man who has it. There are many types of power. The most potent are money, fame, politics, crime and the dark arts. It sounds like your face would keep you from public office. Rock stars are often hideous, but I assume we can forgo music since you mention no talent, I doubt you could even be a one-hit wonder. The tone of your letter marks you as a wimp—you could have used electric shocks to train the dog or used torture to force your mother to go to the dance with you—so a career in organized crime or the dark arts is out.

I suggest you acquire large amounts of money–invent something, pull off a brilliant robbery, knock off a wealthy relative after making them change their will to name you their sole beneficiary. Of course, if it was me, I'd also make sure I was named their soul beneficiary. Sadly, for you I sense nothing of greatness about you, so your efforts might be best focused on trying to win the lottery or seeing if your local school for the blind will let you audit classes.

Also, consider only going out on dates on Halloween.

Dear Cthulhu,

I'm having a major problem with my husband, "Bert". He's always had a roaming eye, but lately, it's gotten out of control. I understand it's a natural instinct to want to look at an attractive person, but does he have to turn his head so fast that I'm surprised he hasn't gotten whiplash? Or howl like a wolf and drool all over himself just because some pretty young thing happens to walk by? It's embarrassing and degrading.

It's a sign of disrespect towards me, our wedding vows, and nine children. I don't think I'll be able to take this much longer.

What should I do?

-Wife Wondering About Wandering Eye in Washington

Dear Wife,

No one, even a lowly human, should have to endure disrespect, especially from one who has made vows lasting until death unto them. Frankly, if one of my followers broke a vow to me, wouldn't hesitate to devour his or her soul slowly, then burp it up and do it all over again.

Now, as anyone who knows me knows, I hate to give credit to the competition, but the words of those Bible thumpers holds the solution to your problem. It says, and I am paraphrasing here, that "if an eye offends you, it is better to pluck it out than... blah blah and so on."

Pluck out one of your mate's eyes. It should teach him a lesson and fried in corn meal makes a tasty snack. Plus, he is still alive to serve you. And if it does it again, pluck out the other and console yourself with the knowledge that it was his own fault.

Also, if cornmeal deep fried eye doesn't thrill you, write me and send $4.95 for my pamphlet for 101 Delicious Eyeball Recipes.

Dear Cthulhu,

My parents got divorced and the judge is making me choose between the two of them. I don't want to live with either one. My father is always either drunk or passed out in a pool of his own vomit. My mother has a revolving door on her bedroom and needs a deli ticket counter to keep track of her "boyfriends". The noises from her room keep me up all hours of the night.

I'm thinking of running away, but I only have fifty bucks saved which won't last me a week on the streets. I don't want to end up whoring on some street corner. Enough of my mother's sleazy "boyfriends" have made it abundantly clear I could do that from the comfort of home.

Can you give me advice? Or lots of money?

-Caught Between a Drunk and a Whore's Place

Dear Caught,

Sadly, your predicament is not a new one. In fact, it is all too common in these sad times, which is why, several years ago, I did something about it. I started a place where young people like yourself, disillusioned or abused by society, could go and live safely. Our doors are open to all, no matter who or why, any time of the day or night.

The name of the place is The Cthulhu Orphanage and All You Can Eat Buffet. I hope to see you soon. Please use the back door.

Dear Cthulhu,

They say in politics it is helpful to know where the bodies are buried. I do. They're in my backyard.

I'm a town councilman and frankly, it has helped my political career immensely. It's not like I did *any of the killing myself, mind you. (Well except for that one hooker, but that was accidental. At least that's my story and I'm sticking to it.) The higher ups in my party were having trouble disposing of problem corpses and I volunteered my yard, as I lived alone and really didn't use it much except for the occasional barbecue in the summer.

I have high fences and soft ground, so it wasn't too hard for the men involved to bury what they had to. The problem is that I recently received a great bribe from a contractor—a beautiful new house—and I plan to move. Which means I will have to sell or rent the house and I'm concerned that the new tenants might stumble across something while putting in a pool or maybe they'll have a dog that buries one bone but unburies several hundred larger ones.

Any suggestions for me?

-Public Servant in Grave Trouble

Dear Public,

There are several options available. The wisest would be to install a tennis or basketball court and pave over the entire yard so that digging will be impossible. Then get together with your cronies and pass some zoning laws that will make sure nobody can ever get rid of the court.

Dear Cthulhu,

I'm a divorced woman. My next-door neighbor and I are very good friends. Recently she and her husband went on a trip and left their two teenage boys home. She asked me to keep an eye on her house and her kids. I said I would.

Things went fine for the first few days, but then one night I was woken up in the middle of the night by loud music. The boys were having a party. I went over immediately to tell them to send everyone home.

That's not what ended up happening. The party went on to dawn. Then they had another one each night, but I was invited to each one. I was the life of the party, especially the first night. Of course, that may have partially been because I didn't change when I woke up and showed up in my nightie.

I sort of ended up playing Mrs. Robinson. Twice. Each couple of hours. My ex was lousy, both as a husband and a lover. These boys were attentive and enthusiastic, plus they don't mind sharing. I figure I'm entitled to a little happiness.

My problem is my friend came back and now I feel guilty about not telling her about the party. Plus, she keeps asking me why her sons are doing so many chores at my house.

What should I do?

-Desperate House Ex-Wife

Dear Desperate,

Telling your friend will only make things worse for you. First, she will never trust you again and she would punish her sons about the party. They, in turn, may feel compelled to tell about your tutoring in old movie seductions. If your state has strict statutory rape laws, you could end up doing time.

Ask yourself if it is worth it. Then make sure you use protection as you won't be getting much by way of child support from a teenager. And keep the blinds drawn while they are doing their so-called chores or the mother may be able to see for herself what is really happening.

Dear Cthulhu,

I'm a twenty-three-year-old woman. My boyfriend "Hank" finally proposed to me. It seems like he took forever to pop the question. I mean we had been dating for nearly four months.

The problem is he's very old fashioned and doesn't know I've been married before. A few times. Actually, seventeen times, but I don't count 14 of them, as I was drunk and managed to get several of them annulled. Plus, one of my ex's is a divorce lawyer and as part of my settlement with him, he represents me in all my future divorces for free.

Hank has no clue about any of this and I think it would devastate him to find out, especially since he thinks I was a virgin when I met him.

What's the best way to handle this so I don't lose Hank?

-The Marrying Kind in Montreal

Dear Marrying,

You do not say if all of your numerous ex-husbands live in the same town as you. If that is the case, the only way to stop him from finding out would be to keep him locked up in the basement or relocate.

Another possibility is changing your entire name after the ceremony. Many states let you do this for free after a marriage. Then dye your hair and have massive amounts of plastic surgery to drastically alter your appearance. Getting Hank to go along with it should not be a problem. Simply tell him you witnessed a mob murder and need to go into hiding. That way you can justify who you allow him to see.

Congratulations on your pending nuptials. And my condolences to Hank.

Dear Cthulhu,

My new favorite column is Dear Cthulhu. I have been single for some time and finally gave in to posting on an online site. At first, it was kind of exciting receiving 75-100 emails a day from potential mates. I have gone out with some, had email sex with others and even fell hard for one particular fella. My question to you is—why are all these 'amazingly' unattached guys here and not out in other places I could find them like at the gym or supermarket?

-Girl in New York City

Dear Girl,

Simple. They are men looking to procreate and they have chosen a way to meet women without having to go through the usual methods, like verifying who they are. The men are probably married or otherwise involved and too cheap or dishonest to use call girls. As for why you cannot find them at the gym or supermarket, it is because they are there with their actual mates who are making sure to keep you and others like you away from their claimed territory.

A question for you, as Cthulhu is apparently not as well versed in human procreation as he thought. How does one have sex with an e-mail? Must you print it out first or are there electrodes you need to hook up to your body? And are you that unattractive that you cannot find someone to look at you directly? And was your e-mail trying to get fresh with Cthulhu and I somehow missed it?

Dear Cthulhu,

Is it true that it's best to date guys before the age of 25? Statistics state that when a guy is over the age of 25 he is either: taken, lying to you that he isn't taken, married, or lying to you that he is divorced.

Please clear this up for me.

-Italian Princess Yvonne they call me!

Dear Italian,

It depends on what you are looking for from the male. Are you looking for enthusiasm and stamina? Then under 25 is better. Are you looking for a mixture of skill and staying power? Try over 25. Are you looking for someone to shower you with gifts and keep things a secret? Try a married man in a mid-life crisis, usually over 45. Looking for gratitude? Try over 55. Looking for someone to keel over after the loving? Try over 95.

Statistics have often been proven by studies as something to be avoided. Human men are lying to you anyway in hopes of procreation. It is only the nature of their lies that differs. If he never wants to go to his place or what he claims is his place charges by the hour, assume he is taken and, if that bothers you, move on.

Of course, by the way that you phrased your question, you may mean your age and that you are planning on dating something other than men starting on your 26th birthday. May I inquire as to what? Women, cucumbers, barnyard animals, house plants, or power equipment? Perhaps Girl will share her e-mail with you.

Dear Cthulhu,

I'm embarrassed by my dog, "Killer". He's a pit bull I bought for protection because I live in a bad neighborhood, but he is the biggest wimp ever. Killer's not only afraid of his own shadow but jumps at his own farts like someone lit a firecracker.

I tried to take him to obedience school in hopes they could teach him some courage, but he hid under my shirt the entire class. The other day he actually barked at my neighbor's guinea pig and I was thrilled until the pig looked at him and he ran away whimpering with his tail between his legs.

I'm thinking about getting rid of him. What else can I do?

-Owner of a Fraidy Dog

Dear Owner,

It sounds like Killer might have suffered abuse in his past. Getting rid of your pet seems rather heartless of you, especially considering the possible abuse. When you took on the responsibilities of ownership of another being, you took on the good and the bad. When one of Cthulhu's human pets ran screaming every time she saw me, I didn't get rid of or kill her. I put the time and the effort into making her behave properly. Now when I enter the room she simply goes into a catatonic stupor. Occasionally she comes out of it long enough for us to play a game of hide and seek. She's so cute when she pretends to faint and play dead when I find her.

Dear Cthulhu,

I've slept with my Teddy every night since I was a little boy, even though my parents say I'm too old. I'm in kindergarten now. The other morning when I woke up, Teddy was gone. I looked everywhere but he disappeared.

I think the monster in my closet ate Teddy, but Daddy says I'm wrong. Can you help me?

-Five in Freeport

Dear Five,

Yes, Cthulhu can help you. Your father is correct. The monster in your closet did not eat Teddy. It was the creature under your bed. And he is hungry again.

Dear Cthulhu,

I work in a physician's office for a cute doctor. As long as I've worked there, I've been hoping for him to make a move on me, but he never had. I figured if he did, I could reel him in, get married which would stop my mother from constantly telling me I should marry a doctor. I could also rub my sister's face in it because she always brags she bagged a doctor, but her husband is only a podiatrist, not a real doctor.

I've been here four years and had given up on him. Recently our office manager left and I had the most seniority so I assumed I would get the promotion. He gave it instead to "Suzy", a new girl who was all of nineteen and I couldn't figure out why until one night I came back to the office to get something I forgot. I got a big surprise instead when I found him taking her temperature with his personal thermometer. Both ways.

I was shocked and upset. I would have gladly played doctor with him to get that promotion. What I want to know is can I sue for sexual discrimination? I mean I wanted to have sex with him and he discriminated against me.

-High and Dry in North Dakota

Dear Dry,

Cthulhu would like to state that he is not a lawyer, but it is my understanding that you cannot sue him for sexual discrimination unless he is having sex with everyone else in the office except for you. Perhaps you should have been more aggressive in luring your boss or perhaps you were too aggressive. I can only conclude that you are less than attractive or at the very least less attractive than your competition. You do not mention the type of doctor you work for. If he is a plastic surgeon perhaps you should have him work on decreasing your ugliness. Maybe you can even get an employee discount.

Dear Cthulhu,

I've always believed in sex, drugs, and rock and roll. It's kind of my religion and I try to get all three at the same time whenever I can. I consider myself a virgin because I've never slept with a regular guy, only serious rock and rollers, singers who can fill a stadium or in a pinch the guys in the band. Except for that one time with that t-shirt guy, but he was an Elvis impersonator on the side. Since he told me he could channel the King and I was really high at the time, I've always counted that as the real thing.

I go from one concert to another. I'm on the backstage list at every major venue and if I'm left off, the guys at the door let me in, figuring maybe I'll sleep with them if they do. That will never happen. It's not my fault they delude themselves and I don't feel bad for taking advantage of them for it. Well, maybe sometimes I do and I flash them a little something to make them feel good about themselves. I'm really a people person at heart.

Lately, I've been pretty exclusive with a rocker who was big back in my Mom's day. Mom lives the same lifestyle I do. She got pregnant with me back when she was 13, but she was a good enough mother to make sure I didn't have to start as late as she did to boff rock stars. It is a little embarrassing when people mistake us as sisters though.

My rocker guy is huge and I don't just mean famous. Not to mention rich. And the things he can do with his... let's just say I'm a happy girl. And to top it all off he proposed marriage and the prenup gives me a million if anything happens. And I'll only be his third wife.

There's just one problem. Back in the day, my Mom knew him in the biblical sense. Normally that wouldn't be an issue. We've slept with a lot of the same rockers, sometimes right after each other or at the same time, but this is different. Mom now claims he's my father, but I think she's just jealous because no rock gods ever proposed to her.

The only way to know for sure is to have both of us tested,

but I think that would kind of ruin the wedding plans. Is it okay to keep this from him? I'm not planning to have kids, so we wouldn't have to worry about three eyed babies or anything. Besides, you should see the stretch marks Mom had from me. She had to get surgery to cut them away, but a side effect from the tightened skin is you really see the definition in her abs. I might have considered getting knocked up in order to trap him into marriage or get some major child support payments, but I don't see the point of going through all that if I'm already married to the guy. I mean, what's the point? Pregnant people look fat and fat girls don't get rock gods. What should I do?

-Rock and Roll Virgin in Raleigh

Dear Rock,

Humans have so many odd taboos—avoiding the eating of human flesh, not committing genocide and the like. Sleeping with your own father seems relatively minor compared to those, especially since he doesn't know and was not the one who raised you. Who will be able to tell? After all, the lot of you look alike.

Cthulhu does recommend you get the paternity test if for no other reason than that way you will know for sure. It can be done without his knowledge. Simply steal his toothbrush or ask for a lock of hair. He'll think it's a quaint romantic gesture. Personally, Cthulhu would ask for the entire scalp—they make excellent coasters, even if the humans that grew the hair tend to object.

However, if you go through with the wedding, do not tell him if he did father you. Save that information for the divorce. Although his farewell gift in the prenuptial agreement is quite generous, Cthulhu believes you will find him much more generous if you threaten to reveal to the media that he married his own daughter. Have no qualms regarding accepting the money. Consider it a combination retroactive child support and early inheritance. Reflect on using some of it to have yourself neutered.

Dear Cthulhu,

I have a dream to be the greatest guitar player who ever lived. The one big thing standing in my way is I'm incredibly lazy and have no desire to practice. I've decided to approach things in a non-traditional manner. Back in the old days, they say certain bluesmen met the devil at the crossroads and sold their souls in order to be able to play. I've hit every major crossroad in my neighborhood, drawn pentacles and lit candles, but nobody showed up to make me an offer, so now I'm turning to you. What can you offer me in exchange for my soul?

-Soul Man in Seattle

Dear Soul,

One measly soul is barely a snack and yours sounds like it is rather stunted. You want Cthulhu to give you something for that? Why would Cthulhu want to? If Cthulhu desired your puny soul, Cthulhu would simply suck it out of your mortal husk.

And the reason the devil hasn't shown up is he doesn't like you or want your soul either, although he's willing to consider it in exchange for granting you the ability to play the ukulele. You are not likely to receive a better offer for what you are offering.

Dear Cthulhu,

I've been dating "Bill" for almost two years. He's been a minor-league pitcher for years and wasn't going anywhere. He was marriage material, but he'd be even more impressive if he was a better ballplayer so I took matters into my own hands and started feeding him oral steroids. I work in a pharmacy and had no problems getting a hold of them. I put them in his evening beer and he was none the wiser.

Within six months he was pitching no-hitters and batting 266. Then he was moved up to the majors and while not a superstar, got local endorsements and an increase in pay. We got married.

Things went bad with the new league policy on steroids. Bill got picked for a random screening. Since he didn't know about it, he filled the cup with his own urine instead of buying clean pee like the rest of his teammates who use performance enhancers.

When the positive result came back, Bill got a ten-day suspension. He hit the roof and starting demanding a re-test. I talked him out of it, but he's bound to be re-tested so I stopped his roid cocktails. His game's suffered and he's gone from first string to second.

I'm torn about what to do. Should I wait until after the next test and restart the steroids? How long do these things stay in someone's system? Should I tell him what I did? If I can't get his game back up, should I leave him? One of his teammates has been hitting on me. I've said no so far, but he gets a higher salary than Bill.

-Ballplayer's Steroid Dealing Wife

Dear Dealing,

What you did was done for your benefit and, to a lesser degree, Bill's. However, many humans would want to punish you for your self-serving actions, as justifiable as they may be. Your husband may be one of them, so I recommend silence.

As for how long the steroids stay in the human bloodstream, Cthulhu would like to state he is not a doctor. Which, Cthulhu would like to state, is a pointless profession. If a human dies, others will just procreate and make more, so why waste time and effort to save something that is so easily replaceable? However, it is my understanding that it stays at least 60 days.

As for when to restart, how about just encouraging him to work harder? Or investing some of his endorsement deals into steroids that won't show up on the testing? Or convincing him that his urine has a rare component that shows a false positive and convincing him to use someone else's liquid waste the next time he has to fill a testing cup.

Finally, I would advise keeping your vows. The odds of the teammate wanting you for more than a few procreative encounters is slim. Right now, you are forbidden fruit and therefore exciting. If suddenly you leave your spouse for him, he will bolt and I doubt Bill would take you back.

Dear Cthulhu,

I have a problem at work. My network administrator "Gill" recently began using my login and password to order things from the company's warehouse. Apparently, they have nothing at all to do with work but are for his personal use. He's been taking them home, assuming I will get the blame. It seems Gill's holding a grudge because I've been sleeping with his wife. I wouldn't even know if she didn't tell me. Apparently, he's been hoarding the stuff in his garage.

I checked my account logs and the supplies have added up. There have been several computers, scanners, office furniture, office supplies, and several dinners from the executive dining room. I'm not even an executive.

I'm worried that when the hire-ups in the company find out, they'll fire me. I don't want to be fired and I want Gill to get in trouble for this.

How can I do it?

-Nervous in Nevada

Dear Nervous,

First off, is there anything from the company that you would like? If so, wait until Gill goes home. Because of your liaisons with his wife, I'm sure you already have his comings and goings memorized. Go to his computer and log in as yourself and order away. The network will register the transaction as having occurred at his station. Undoubtedly, he's been using your computer while you have been using his wife.

Next, hide your ill-gotten gain in a storage rental facility. Pay with cash and use a phony name if possible. Rub off any serial numbers.

Once that's taken care of, take your concerns directly to the executives. Lie and tell them you saw him taking the stuff to his garage. That should get them to investigate. Hopefully, your company uses time clocks and you were not clocked in went he did the other orders. Clock out before you place your order. It should be enough to back up your story and probably get a search warrant, which will get Gill fired and incarcerated. And you will have new stuff, his wife, and the satisfaction of beating him at his own game.

Dear Cthulhu,

I am known for my taste in jewelry. All my friends beg me to tell them where I shop, but I never do. How could I, since I steal it all? My problem is I get it while on the job and I work doing makeup at a funeral home.

I help seal up the coffins before they go to the cemetery and slide the bling out then. I've done it for a decade without having a problem. That was until I got stupid. I took a custom-made broach off an elderly woman and wore to a party. One of the woman's grandchildren was there and accused me of stealing it. I said I bought it at a yard sale, which is when she brought up the fact that it was a one of a kind.

She's offering to keep quiet if I give it to her. Apparently, all the women in her family were promised the broach by the woman and there was so much fighting over it, that they decided the only way to keep peace was to bury it with the grandmother.

Of course, if I give it to her I'm basically admitting to robbing the dead and that could get me fired. If I don't, she'll turn me in and I'll still get fired and probably go to jail.

I've been thinking about killing her and stuffing her in a casket with another body when I seal a coffin. I'd probably never get caught. What do you think?

-Pre-Grave Robber in Phoenix

Dear Robber,

Your problem is of your own making. You were sloppy, wearing the purloined jewelry in the same town as the dead woman's family. You should have broken it down for the jewelry and melted the metal.

As for your plan, Cthulhu would once again like to state that people should not kill people. That task is reserved for Cthulhu alone.

There is a way around this. Simply dig up the woman's body and replace the jewelry. Then let the woman tell everyone. If it comes to the point of a trial, you can insist the DA exhume the body. You will be cleared and have the way paved for a libel lawsuit against the woman. With the money, you could start buying your own jewelry.

Dear Cthulhu,

My husband and I are newlyweds and we have a hairy situation, namely my husband's back. Sleeping with "Harry" is like sleeping with a sheep dog. I invested in 400 thread count sheets made out of Egyptian cotton and every morning they look like a barber shop floor. Harry sheds enough every night to make a toupee, yet he never seems to get less furry. For a while, I was afraid he might be a werewolf, but the full moon didn't change anything.

He refuses to shave or wax, but I'm not sure I can handle this for much longer. The situation is putting my marriage in jeopardy. What can I do?

-Back-haired in a Corner

Dear Corner,

Did you forget to look at your husband before you married him? Was he not furry then? If so, you have every right to ask him to get rid of the hair. If he was, what did you think would happen after you married him—that he'd be struck by lightning and it would make all his hair fall out via natural electrolysis?

You took a vow and should honor it. However, humans tend not to place stock in promises, so your best bet is to take matters into your own hands. Seduce him into getting rid of the hair - start out by bringing different things to bed with you while wearing lingerie. First, chocolate, then whipped cream, and finally shaving cream and a razor. My experience is most men while in the heat of the moment will do things to get what they lust for that they would never do at other times.

Dear Cthulhu,

I'm normally a very quiet guy. I don't go out much and my dating history with women was bleak unless you count when I went to my senior prom with my twelve-year-old cousin. Of course, after less than an hour she left me for one of the guys in the band.

That all changed a week ago when I met "Jane". She was a freshman at the local college. She was blond and built like a centerfold. Jane was even a cheerleader in high school.

I was out at a local bar and when she picked me up, I could barely believe it. I was in heaven. A gorgeous girl was interested in me. We had a whirlwind romance. I took her out to all the best fast food restaurants, sent her a dozen carnations every day—you know swept her off her feet.

Then at the end of the week, it happened—we did the deed. I rocked her world for a good four minutes! I know, because every minute I stopped to look at the clock. I've got to tell you, I finally felt like a man, which at 44 was probably long overdue.

The next day is when the problems started. I called her at least twenty times that morning and another thirty that afternoon and she didn't return a single one. Things went on like that for another three days until she showed up at my apartment, a scarf wrapped around her head and sunglasses on.

She wanted to talk to me. Jane was pledging a sorority and her hazing included having to sleep with me. She said that everything that happened meant nothing. In fact, she was embarrassed about what happened and she never wanted to be seen with me again. I didn't even rate the "let's be friends" speech. No, she told me I was creeping her out and to stop calling or she'd call the cops.

Looking back, I should have insulted her or spit in her face, then yelled at her to get out. Maybe tell her how much money I was going to make selling the video of her naked on the internet. (She hadn't noticed the camera.) But I tend to follow my emotions first and my head second, so I kind of ended up strangling her.

My emotions still running the show, I decided the best way to get rid of the body was to cut her up into little pieces and flush them down the toilet. I tried my gonzo knives. They may cut through a tin can, but human bones are another thing. I ended up buying a hacksaw and an industrial size food processor.

The disposal worked pretty good, up until the end. I admit I got lazy and started putting larger pieces down the crapper than I should have, but I had been slicing and flushing for fourteen hours straight and I was tired.

I ended up plugging the toilet. I tried plunging, even poured a gallon of Liquid Plunger down, but nothing happened. I'm worried that if I call a plumber, he'll figure out what happened. At the very least he'll ask why the water in the bowl is purple. (It's normally blue mixed with all the blood and it turned that color.)

What can I do to clean out my pipes?

-Backed Up In Baltimore

Dear Backed Up,

Cthulhu would again like to state his policy that humans should not kill people, Cthulhu should. But as it is too late in this case, I order you to never do it again and I will overlook it this once.

I suggest going to your local hardware store and purchasing a tool called a snake. You will be able to work it through the pipe and it should clear the blockage.

I also suggest canceling your plans to sell the video on the web. It would eventually lead law enforcement to your door asking questions you would not want to answer.

Dear Cthulhu,

My daughter "Bertha" is big for her age. Actually, she's big for any age at 6'3" and 200 pounds. She's a football fanatic and wanted to play on her high school team. My ex-wife, who has custody, is a lawyer and helped her sue the school district for sexual discrimination. Unfortunately, they won and Bertha got to join the team. Worse, she tried out for quarterback and got it.

Then Bertha led the team to its first division title in 17 years. The state championship is next week.

My problem is the guys at work are ribbing me mercilessly about my daughter and calling her all manner of unflattering names, questioning her sexuality and mocking her looks and her size. Unlike my daughter, I'm small, weighing in at 120 pounds and 5'4". I feel obligated to defend my daughter and I'm not a good fighter. I've been beaten up sticking up for her after nearly every home game. With each game she wins the beatings get worse—most of my co-workers are fans of opposing teams. I'm worried that I'll be hospitalized if she wins the state championship.

I've been debating asking her to not play. I've thought about drugging her, but I just can't do that to my own daughter. Plus, if she wins she's a shoe-in for a college scholarship. (The last three quarterbacks who won the state championship got at least five scholarship offers from the same universities. If they don't make the same offer, my ex- already has the papers ready to file the discrimination lawsuits.)

I love my daughter and want the best for her, but can't deal with another beating. What should I do?

-Wussy Dad in Wisconsin

Dear Wussy,

You could simply agree with your co-workers to avoid the beatings, but Cthulhu admires your defense of your offspring. Cthulhu does not understand it but admires it.

Your solution is easy. Tell everyone it is bring your daughter to work day and bring Bertha. Tell her what your co-workers have been saying about her and let her beat them up instead.

Dear Cthulhu,

I recently bought a new car. I should preface this by mentioning I'm a little OCD. I love the car, but ever since I got it, I haven't been able to sleep because I've been so paranoid about something happening to the car. I have the alarm set to maximum sensitivity, but since I always park in the back reaches of my work parking lot, I never hear it. Same at the mall and the supermarket.

I'm even worried about a bird leaving droppings on my car. It's gotten to the point where I started feeding stray cats to keep the feathered pooping machines away. I even stole and buried my neighbor's bird feeder. She's retired and a bird watcher so, unfortunately, she keeps replacing them but blames it on the neighborhood kids. So far, I've buried five of them in my backyard. Also, her pine tree is starting to grow over my driveway and it might drip sap so I was thinking of sneaking out at night to cut it down. I wouldn't have to if I wasn't so worried about it falling on my car.

Worse, my co-workers know about my paranoia and feed into it. When they come in from their smoking breaks, they tell me they saw someone near my car or say they heard metal on metal and think the car next to me may have scratched mine. That means I have to leave my desk and go out and check my car. It takes me a while because I have to check the entire body carefully; the windows, the tires and even underneath to make sure nobody planted a bomb. No, I don't know anyone who would have a reason to do it, but it could happen. A lot of cars look alike. The problem is the checking takes so long that I'm missing time at my job, which is upsetting my boss. My co-workers do this at least a few times a day, so if they won't stop I may get fired. That means I won't be able to make the payments, which means they'll repossess the car, which makes me worry more. It's at the point where I don't sleep because I'm listening for the car alarms and the flutter of bird wings.

What can I do?

-Auto Obsessed in Albany

Dear Auto,

Since you appear unable to control your obsessive urges, you need to learn to control your environment. Your actions with the cats and taking the bird feeders are steps in the right direction, just not enough. If you are that worried simply buy a car cover or in your case, several inexpensive ones that you can dispose of if the birds target it successfully. Or purchase a carport which can be ordered from most auto supply stores and put it up in your driveway.

Accept that your co-workers are getting enjoyment out of making you jump through their hoops and stop it. Video baby monitors are inexpensive and easily obtained and can run on battery power. Get a multi-channel model and leave the cameras on your dashboard and rear window, each tilted toward opposite sides so you can get a good view of your vehicle. Leave the video monitor on your desk so you can glance at it while still being able to get your work done. Given the nature of your office mates, I would advise taking the monitor with you when you leave the desk for bathroom and lunch breaks or you will find it missing on your return. Plus, with batteries, you can always see your car, even at a store. And with some of the models you can transmit your voice, so you can tell any actual offenders to back away from your car.

Of course, you totally forgot to figure in car thieves. And joy riders and vandals. Not to mention teenagers with keys in their hands and mischief in their hearts. Plus, there are people who stand on overpasses and drop stuff on cars underneath them. And dogs walking by and marking their territory on your tires. Not to mention frozen restroom waste dropped from flying airplanes that can hit with the force of a small meteorite. But I would hate for you to have more to worry about, so forget I mentioned anything.

Dear Cthulhu,

I am a twelve-year-old boy in middle school. I like girls but I'm too shy to talk to them. Most of my friends are starting to get girlfriends and when they make out, sometimes the girls leave a hickey. It's like a badge of honor among the guys. I have to admit, I was feeling left out. I'm not really popular so I thought if people thought I had a girlfriend they'd think I was cool and I'd move up the social ladder, but like I said I'm too shy to speak to girls so I came up with an idea.

When nobody was home, I took my mom's vacuum and put the smallest attachment on the hose and held it up to the back of my neck. My hair is long enough to cover it so my parents didn't see. The next day at school, I got a lot of attention showing off my hickey. Unfortunately, they all wanted to know who it was. I played coy and said it was an older girl who didn't go to our school.

It worked so good, girls started talking to me. I could hardly believe it, but when the hickey faded, so did the attention. I got the vacuum out again. And again. The more I marked my body, the more people paid attention to me. I admit it got a little out of control. At one point, I had more red and purple marks on me than unblemished skin. One of my classmates told a teacher, who told my guidance counselor. She called my parents. Let me tell you there is nothing more awkward than sitting in an office with your parents and a counselor asking you to explain why you have hickeys all over your body and them demanding to know who did it. I thought about saying Hoover but worried they'd think I was being molested by a dead president and lock me up. I thought about telling them I did it to myself, but I couldn't bring myself to say it. Instead, I made up a story about a smoking hot neighbor around the corner. We had spent the summer weekends peeking through her fence to watch her sunbathe and I thought about her a lot. I really wished she had put the marks on me and sometimes when I used the vacuum, I'd think of her in that bikini.

I thought that would be the end of it, but the cops arrested her.

I had never heard of statutory rape, but apparently, it has nothing to do with humping a sculpture. "Hotty" denied it of course, but it didn't do any good. I tried to tell them I wouldn't testify, but with these charges, I don't need to. They took pictures of my body with all the vacuum marks and are using them as evidence.

I don't want her to go to jail, but I won't tell the truth either. For the first time in years, my parents are really paying attention to me. My Dad is taking me to ballgames, Mom is baking every day. I go to counseling three times a week. I mention any problem and the shrink talks to people to fix it for me. Word got out on the local news that I was doing Hotty and girls are throwing themselves at me. I've had sex with five girls in the last week, three of them are in high school and two jumped me at the same time. And whenever I go to drop off things at one of my mom's friends, she always seems to be coming to the door in her underwear. To top it all off, I seem to be the most popular guy in school now. I'm in heaven.

So, the question is, what do I do about Hotty?

-Sticky Hickey Stud in El Paso

Dear El,

Without you recanting, they will most likely put Hotty in jail and she will have to register as a sex offender when she gets out. Not a pleasant outlook for an innocent woman. If you had any money, you could hire her the best attorney in the state, but it is unlikely your allowance would cover a consultation, let alone a trial. If your conscience allows this, then, by all means, maintain your silence on the matter.

And regarding your liaisons with members of the opposite sex—I realize that you have heard it again and again in school and on TV, but use protection. The last thing anyone wants is for you to procreate.

Dear Cthulhu,

I am eight years old and have lost my best friend Wags. We've looked everywhere, but haven't been able to find him.

Mr. Cthulhu, I'm desperate. Do you know where my dog is?

-Lonely in LA

Dear Lonely,

As a matter of fact, I do. A pity you did not actually ask me to tell you where your dog was. Write in again if you really want to know, but I recommend you hurry. Poor Wags does not have much time left.

Dearest Cthulhu,

Why haven't you returned any of my calls? After the weekend we spent together in Vegas, I thought we meant something to each other.

You told me you loved me. Call me, please.

-Love Sick in Las Vegas

Dear Lovesick,

I may have told you I loved you, but you told me you were a virgin. So now we both know we lied.

We had a good time, but that is all it was. Deal with it, get over it and move on with your life. Just leave Cthulhu alone

Dear Cthulhu,

You heartless, soul-sucking scum. You made promises, we made plans. Did I mean so little to you that you can throw all that away, including what I did to your little tentacles?

-Love Sick in Las Vegas

Dear Lovesick,

Thank you for your kind words. Yes, you did mean that little to me and what else does one do with trash except throw it away? And Cthulhu's tentacles are not little.

Dear Cthulhu,

I'm late, so I went to the doctor. Guess what? I'm pregnant and you're the daddy, so get ready to pay up, tentacle boy.

-Love Sick in Las Vegas

Dear Sick,

How cruel of you. When you said you were late, I hoped you meant as in dead.

So much for your claims you were on the pill.

As for your paternity claims, prove it.

Dear Cthulhu,

I've begun to accept that you don't love me anymore and I'm learning to live with the rejection, but how can you reject your own flesh and blood?

-Love Sick in Las Vegas

Dear Sick,

While it might be comforting to know I have a child out there in case I ever need a transfusion or heart transplant, I have yet to see any proof.

Dear Cthulhu,

It's time for you to stop being a deadbeat dad and step up to the plate. I'm expecting at least $2,000 a month child support plus a college fund for your son, Cthulhu Jr.

I've enclosed a picture of your offspring as undeniable proof of his parentage.

When can I expect the first check?

-Love Sick in Las Vegas

Dear Sick,

I have seen the picture of what you claim is my spawn. That is not my son. You madam, put a diaper on an octopus to perpetrate your fraud in the first picture and in the second have stapled a squid to a doll's face.

I have had enough of your nonsense. I will indeed step up to the plate, and you and my so-called son will be on it, slow roasted with apples in your mouths.

Have a Dark Day.

PATRICK THOMAS is the award-winning author of almost 40 books including the beloved fantasy humor Murphy's Lore series, which includes *Tales From Bulfinche's Pub, Fools' Day, Through The Drinking Glass, Shadow Of The Wolf, Redemption Road, Bartender Of The Gods, Nightcaps, Empty Graves, The Mug Life* — as well as the future space adventures S*tartenders* and *Constellation Prize.*

The Murphy's Lore After Hours spin-offs star the half pixie/ogre Terrorbelle (*Fairy With A Gun, Fairy Rides The Lightning* and *Terrorbelle The Unconquered);* the former demon-possessed serial killer Agent Karver of the Department of Mystic Affairs *(Dead To Rites, Rites of Passage);* the cursed magí Hex *(By Darkness Cursed and By Invocation Only);* Vince Argus, the Soul For Hire *(Greatest Hits);* and Negral, a forgotten Sumerian god who works as Hell's Detective *(Lore & Dysorder* and *Bullets & Brimstone).*

Co-Written with John French and Diane Raetz, his Mystic Investigators paranormal mystery series includes *Mean Streets* and the omnibus editions *Shadows & Bullets & Brimstone* and *Once Upon In Crime. Assassin's Ball,* his first mystery, is also co-written with John French.

His works include the steampunk *As The Gears Turn* and the space epic *Exile & Entrance.* He co-edited *New Blood* and *Hear Them Roar* and was an editor for the magazines *Fantastic Stories of the Imagination* and *Pirate Writings.*

Patrick's darkly humorous advice column Dear Cthulhu has been running since 2005 and includes the collections *Have A Dark Day, Good Advice For Bad People, Cthulhu Knows Best, Cthulhu Happens, Cthulhu Explains It All* and *What Would Cthulhu Do?* Dear Cthulhu appears monthy on the radio show *Destinies: The Voice of Science Fiction* which is hosted by Dr. Howard Margolin.

His short stories have been featured in over sixty anthologies and more than forty-five print magazines.

A number of his books were part of the props department of the CSI television show and Nightcaps was even thrown at a suspect's head. His urban fantasy Fairy With A Gun had been optioned for film and TV by Laurence Fishburne's Cinema Gypsy Productions. Top Men Productions has turned his Soul For Hire Story, *Act of Contrition,* into a short film.

Please drop by www.patthomas.net or follow him at I_PatrickThomas at Twitter or www.facebook.com/PatrickThomasAuthor to learn more.

Help is only a Rainbow *Away*...

"Mix Gaiman's American Gods and Robinson's Callahan's Crosstime Saloon on Prachett's Discworld and you get an idea of Thomas' Murphy's Lore." -David Sherman, author of STARFIST and Demontech

"ENTERTAINING, INVENTIVE AND DELIGHTFULLY CREEPY." -JONATHAN MABERRY, New York Times and Bram Stoker Award Winning Author

"SLICK... ENTERTAINING." - Paul Di Filippo, ASIMOV'S

"HUMOR, OUTRAGEOUS ADVENTURES, & SOME CLEVER PLOT TWISTS." -Don D'Ammassa, SCIENCE FICTION CHRONICLE

PATRICK THOMAS

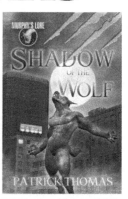

DOWN THESE
MEAN STREETS
of Magic & Monsters walk the

MYSTIC INVESTIGATORS

CPSIA information can be obtained
at www.ICGtesting.com
Printed in the USA
JSHW020202130323
38846JS00003B/195